Clint Faraday
book 55
A Vacation to Die For

Tammy Sheridan, a Valley Girl, like, you know, those in the eighties, won a vacation to die for in a contest. First stop was Cancun, second stop, Managua, third stop, Bocas del Toro, forth stop, Cartagena, fifth stop, Rio de Janiero.

She didn't make the fourth stop.

Tammy was considered a little weird, but was liked. No one had any reason to kill her.

Somebody did.

Contents

About the author

CD Moulton has traveled extensively over much of the world both in the music business, where he was a rock guitarist, songwriter and arranger and in an import/export business. He has been everything from a bar owner to auto salvage (junkyard) manager, longshoreman to high steel worker, orchid grower to landscaper, tropical fish farmer to commercial fisherman. He started writing books in 1983 and has published more than 350 books as of January 1, 2023. His most popular books to date are about research with orchids, though much of his science fiction and fantasy work has proven popular. He wrote the CD Grimes, PI series, and the Det. Nick Storie series, Clint Faraday series, and many other works.

He now resides in Gualaca, Chiriqui, Panamá, where he writes books, plays music with friends, does research with orchids and medicinal plants. He has lately become involved in fighting for the rights of the indigenous people, who are among his closest friends, and in fighting the extreme corruption in the courts and police in Panamá.

He offers the free e-book, *Fading Paradise*, that explains what he has been through because of the corruption.

CD is the discoverer of the Chadam Protocol for curing cancer.

Facebook page Ambrosia peruviana for cancer.

Tammy Fordham Sheridan answered her pink custom-designed Blackberry. It was a bad time for chat, but only her very closest few friends had the number.

"Tammy? Wow, girlfriend! You won!" Leslee Albins cried.

"I did? Like, what?"

"The vacation! You remember! It was, like, late last Saturday night when we were, like, in Cosmosation! You bought that ticket from Eddie Baines. One of those things that, like, cure AIDS or whatever. You know."

"Beddie Edie? I, like, maybe, remember giving him ten dollars for something.

"A vacation?"

"It's that, like, some charity smuggin thing, A Vacation to Die For. Your name won. You go to five, like, special exotic ports, all paid and a hundred dollars a day for, like, things."

"Well, what ports? I don't ... but it might be, like, exotic en fin."

"Let's see. Cancún – I was there. Clicking at dusk til. Managua. Big night club sort of thing, like. Bocas del Toro? I never ... it's that place like Key West! Sher can inform. Was. With Phil and that Arturo hood. Last year. Very surfy. Cartagena. Sort of, like vacationy, family shit, you know? Change. Rio. You liked Rio. It ends there at, like, that Mardi Gras or whatever kinda thing. First class acommodos all the way.

"Fly out of LAX Monday! Like, get your ass in motion, girl! Enjoy!"

"Oh, well. Might. Dregsville around here."

They chatted. Tammy decided she wouldn't go, then changed her mind. She could always come back if it was dullsville or whatever. She liked the Latin guys. The ones who didn't think they owned you. Not the macho facade. She could live without that, like, crap. Arturo Finch turned out to be like that, but some of Sherri's friends were, like, gross!

Bocas del Toro. Panamá. That place where her sister, Sherri, said that Indian was the best she every laid. Guillermo, that was it. She would look him up. Sherri had good taste in men.

This might be fun! She did like to get away from the same old same old all the time. Lately, life was, like, b-o-r-r-i-n-g-g.

She could try some of those things she bought to wear to parties and never did. Let loose on a vacation. Why have super boobs if you don't, like, flaunt them?

Cancún was Cancún. She'd been there. It was fun, but three nights was, like, one too many. Managua was different than she expected. She would have liked it if she were a guy. Lots of hookers and everything was cheap.

She flew into Bocas Town on Isla Colón at four thirty on Monday. This place had better be better than Managua, but it would have to be if Sherri liked it.

She got off the plane and stretched. It wasn't the kind of flight she would prefer, but she could understand that the island wasn't big enough for a proper airport where the big jets could land.

She went to baggage. Sherri had been right about the Indians. She could just die for skin like that! She wanted to touch the men. Sherri said their skin really was like soft satin! It sure looked it! That black hair and the sexy eyes that looked ready for bed! Sherri said they kept the promise!

Oh, that one was pure, like, *gorgeous*! He looked at her and smiled with the most perfect teeth she ever saw!

"Can I help you with your luggage or to find your hotel?"

God! Thank you Jesus! He speaks English!

"I, like, would ... yes. Thanks. I'm Tammy."

"Guillermo. Do you have a hotel reservation, Tammy?"

"Oh, like certain, you know. Tropical Suites."

"Very nice. You'll like it. Deck on the water and all that. Famous people stay there. Are you one?"

"A people? Yes. Famous, I wish!"

"I think you'll be fun. California?"

"Uh-huh. It's that, like, obvious?"

"Like, fer shur!" He laughed. She couldn't help laughing herself.

He took her to the hotel and helped her find her room. She just couldn't stop herself from touching his arm. The skin really was as satiny as Sherri said! This was the prize stud! The very same identical one! She didn't like the idea of seconds to her own sister, like, but this was a, like, special kind of thing!

"I think you met my sister a year or so ago? Sherri Sheridan?"

"Sherri? Ah, yes! You look like her, some. You're better looking, but please don't tell her I said so."

They laughed. "Are you free for dinner?" she asked.

"I'm not free for anything. There aren't many ways for a man to make a living here. I try to be honest with people. I'm a whore."

"How, like, refreshing! Most men are, but not many admit it!

"I have, like, oodles of money, and this trip is paid for, so what time will I pick you up?"

"You already did!"

She loved it! He was for a good time and this was his living.

She ran her hand down his arm. He pulled her close and kissed her. It was the sexiest kiss she could remember! Like, bazookas! She'd bet the farm he made a damned good living! She'd bet the farm he was as good in bed as Sherri said!

She said she'd be ready about seven if that was suitable?

He would be there. She would find he wasn't an expensive date and that he knew all the best places – besides the ones on her.

As soon as he left she got out her phone. It rang three times at the number she punched on the speed dial.

"Hello? Tammy?" Leslee answered.

"My god! This really is a vacation to die for! That guy Sherri told us about, you know, the Indian? Guillermo?

"I met him! He's going to dinner with me and we're going to have the best night of my life! He's, like, *gorgeous*! And he's out front that he's, like, a whore.

"I never could understand why a man would pay a whore before! Now I know, like, fer shur! God, he's beautiful! And, like, he's honest and fun and I got lost in his eyes and I'm like a virgin right now! God! I'm so scared I won't, like, measure up, you know?"

"Girl, if he's like Sherri said, I'm so jealous I could, like, strangle you! Really? I mean, *really*?"

"Really real real, Girlfriend! Picture time! I'll bet he won't blink if I, like, want him naked!

"God, do I want him naked!"

They laughed. Tammy rang off and went to the shower. She was going to look better than she ever had before! This was going to be the best night of her life!

She was, like, fifty miles from being a virgin, but she was as nervous as one. He was to *die* for!

Tammy snuggled even closer, if that was even possible, to Guillermo. The night had been even more fantasmagoric than she'd fantasized!

He was, like, a god! It wasn't possible for a mere human being to be even half that good! Or that handsome. Or that open.

He had taken her to several places for the native foods and for fun in the native bars. She thought she would have to spend a thousand dollars, but the whole night was less than fifty!

He knew everybody. It was obvious that he had been to bed with all those sexy women. She wouldn't be surprised if he'd been to bed with more than a few of the men – the Indios (they called the native people Indios here). They all hugged him like it.

Well, they were a touching people. They all hugged her when he introduced them. A whole body hug. Tight, like, and it was only partly because she was a gringa and sorta blond. They seemed to be, like, really affectionate with each other as well as with her.

Sherri said they looked at things different. Maybe they just touched a lot.

She was about to, like, slide out of bed, but Guillermo woke up and pulled her to him. She said she had to use the bathroom, so he went with her. They got in the shower and she did things she never thought she'd do. Ever. She loved every picosecond of it!

They went to breakfast at a place called Don Chicho's, though that wasn't the name on it. It was the only place open that early.

That early? She never ever got up before nine thirty! It was only seven!

She couldn't remember ever feeling so very damned *good*!

Guillermo had to go to Isla San Cristóbal. He

would be back by five. She would take the bus to Boca del Drago and be back for him.

She never got back.

"Clint? Sergio here, in Bocas. Are you on the comarca?"

"On the way to Chiriqui Grande. Why?"

"I have a murder that I can't figure. It's not the type of thing that anyone here would do because she didn't know anyone here before last night. Guillermo spent the night with her and said she was sort of flaky, but really a good person."

"Why me?"

"She was from California. Guillermo said he was with her sister a little over a year ago. Everyone with them called the sister a Valley Girl. She was very much like her sister.

"Clint, if there was even a small hint that anyone here would kill her, I can't find it. You're the only one I know who might make something of the mess."

"Okay. I'm a little bored with perfection at the moment. I'll run over there and see what I can find. You know the important things."

"Yes. First thing was to secure her room and the safety box in her name even before they brought her back from Drago. That's where she was killed.

She was strangled with a piece of polypropylene rope."

"No more than ninety five percent of the people here have that laying around. Should be easy!"

"Picture a fist with the middle finger erect!"

Clint called his wife, Tyna, to say there was another murder on Isla Colón. He didn't know when he'd get back.

"Hmm. The Darien, east, then Bocas, west. Can't say you don't cover the whole country!

"Get rice and flour for Mom while you're in Bocas."

Clint went past Chiriqui Grande and on to the islands. He docked at his deck in his house on the island and talked a few minutes with Janet Storie. Her husband, Nick Storie had met Clint and family and once stayed with them on the comarca. Nick had a place on Martinique, but preferred Bocas. The people were a lot easier to get along with here. Nick was with Judi Lum, Clint's neighbor there in Bocas Town, visiting with a big gangster from the states or some such thing. Nick knew the biggest of the big.

Clint remembered his invitation for them to stay there. They took care of the place. He almost never spent time there anymore. Janet said Cole and Nicole (her daughter was Nicole, as was Clint's) were off to Drago to surf.

"I wish I'd remembered you were here! Nick could help Sergio with the murder!"

Janet laughed. "Another working vacation! No thanks!"

He chatted awhile, then went to the police station where his old friend, chief of violent crimes there, met him. They went to a new restaurant for lunch. Sergio filled him in with what they knew.

She was from California. She had won some kind of dream vacation. This was the forth stop. She didn't know anyone here. She spent the night with their good friend, Guillermo. She went to Drago on the bus. She was found four hours later by some mangroves near the beach. She was strangled with a piece of half inch polypropylene rope. Black. Her room at the Suites was sealed immediately, as was her safe box. Dr. Arrends had the body at the morgue. She had a sister, who had been notified. She was in Modesto, California, and would be there on the morning flight from PMA.

They talked about other things, then went to the Suites to carefully search her room. They got the things from the locked box: passport, ticket to Cartagena and another to Rio. Two hundred fifty thousand dollar insurance policy made out to her sister. Some fine jewelry.

There was nothing. She kept a diary, but Clint

saw little new there. It was almost boring.

He read the last page, a short note or two: *Flew in Bocas and met Sherri's 'Oh, Wow!' Guillermo. He really real real **is**!!!! Tonight with him!!!!!*

Surfers just like Pismo & SD. Same ones. Borrrring!

"I wonder if she meant that literally?" Clint asked of no one.

"What?" From Sergio.

"Same ones."

"You don't make sense. You seldom do."

They finished and headed for the station. They'd have to wait for the sister to know if there was anything else to hang onto this. It was going to be a hard case no matter what. The two hardest kinds of cases were when a lot of people had a motive or when no one seemed to have one.

Sherri Sheridan got off the flight with a rather handsome sort. Surfer type. She was pretty, but not quite to the standard of her sister if the photos were accurate. Clint had talked with Guillermo for awhile, waiting for the flight to land. Guillermo would remember Sherri.

He did. He went to hug her and say he was very sorry they had to meet again under these circumstances. Tammy had seemed to be a special kind of person. She reminded him of her little sister the minute he saw her.

She introduced Eddie Baines, the person who had sold her sister the ticket that won the vacation. He said it was just some charity thing his buddy, Phil Vanderhaven, was selling to help with an AIDS hospice they were building in LA. All the group bought a ticket. They did that kind of thing for their friends. Everybody was well-off enough that it didn't hurt. If they wanted a vacation, they took it. This was a lark. They usually didn't even know who won anything. This was the first time they had anyone in their little group win anything, not that it mattered.

"It was a vacation to die for," Eddie said.

"Then she met Guillermo and told Les he was to die for, then she.... Oh, God!" Sherri cried. "The sheriff said she was murdered? I can't believe it! No one would, like, kill Tammy! Everybody liked her!"

"Phil will be all to pieces. He sold the tickets, really. He was kind of, like, wanting to get a, like, more permanent relationship with her," Eddie said. "He couldn't make up his mind if he would, like, marry her or you!"

"Oh, Phil's, like, too emotional. Date you a few times and think he was in love. He's a nice enough guy, and, like, a maybe," Sherri replied. "I'm not ready for that thing yet.

"This isn't what we're here for. Like, ... I've gotta quit saying that. It's how we talk at home.

"Where do we go? What do we do?"

"Wait. She was staying at the Tropical Suites," Sergio answered. "We can take your things there, then we can try to find some kind of reason for this. She didn't know anyone here except for Guillermo for one night. We can't find a trace of motive or a suspect."

"We'll take my boat to Drago as soon as you're ready," Clint suggested. "She was killed there. Maybe you'll spot someone. She must have. Someone who's not supposed to be here or who had motive from California."

They agreed to that. It was a starting place. They didn't have one until now.

Sergio took them to the Suites while Clint went to get his boat. He picked them up at the dock at the Suites and they headed for Boca del Drago and the surfer crowd.

Clint was still considering the diary and the notation that they were the same surfers. Did she mean it literally? Did she know any of them personally? Was it simply a generic statement?

That had to be cleared up. Clint particularly wanted to know if anyone had unexpectedly checked out yesterday or this morning. That could prove very telling.

They chatted about California on the way. It seemed they were a little clique of friends who were stuck back in the time of the valley girls, fifteen years ago. It reminded Clint of people he knew who were still in the hippie era. There were quite a few of those in Panamá.

The ride was pleasant. There was a slight chop, but nothing to affect Clint's boat. He came into the bay side to avoid the waves on the Caribbean side and docked at the hotel dock there. They got out and Sherri suggested they go to the hotel restaurant. She hadn't eaten anything since she got up.

They ordered a light late lunch and watched the people. Clint asked Vanda, their waitress, if she'd noted Tammy.

"The dead girl? I think she was in here with a surfer. Blond and kind of handsome. I couldn't identify him. He was just a gringo surfer. They all tend to look alike after awhile. They're not interested in me except as a waitress. I'm not interested in them except as clients. If he came in here a few more times, I'd remember, because that means tips."

"Tammy was a surfer. I'm not very good at it," Sherri said. "Eddie doesn't do much, but he's kind of, like – I promised not to talk like that!

"Tammy would know surfers from almost

everywhere. She had the same psych kind of way about her. She was popular. She probably just met someone she'd seen before, but that could mean anything or nothing. I know she was always saying she met someone or other from Hawaii or Australia or whatever back home."

"I think that short girl with the long black hair is from Hawaii," Eddie said. "Her name's ... Sydney Lindy or Sydney Lindsay. I met her in SD on the beach. A competition sort of thing. She's from Australia.

"Say! Maybe she saw Tammy here!"

"Find out!" Sergio ordered. Eddie got up and went to a slender pretty girl and talked for a bit, then came back to say she had seen Tammy on the beach when she got off the bus, but she was with Hilo Hank and had just waved. She was talking with some girl from the bus. A native by the looks of her.

Clint told Sergio to wander around with the two to see if they spotted anyone else. He had to use his computer for a few things. He had an idea.

"Where are all the surfers from?"

"And did any leave yesterday or this morning. I also want to investigate some other things. Something doesn't fit here. I can't see what it is, but someone said something...."

"One of those things that nag, but you don't

know what or why?"

"Exactly! Surfers travel with names like Hawaii Hank. Most of them haven't got a clue as to real names."

"So! California Carl or San Diego Sam might be here?"

"Uh-huh. Also note that Sherri and Eddie look like typical surfers. She isn't and he's just under the wire. We might be looking for a surfer who isn't."

"Isn't a surfer. You don't get me this time!"

"I'm going to spend some time trying to find the worm in this barrel of apples."

"Knock it off! I'll talk later. Maybe we can spot someone. There's one thing that will give the one not a surfer away, I think."

Clint nodded. The surfers were all tanned. He'd seen two already who weren't tanned, but they didn't look like surfers either. Someone with a surfer handle and no tan would be a good bet to be a phony if not the one they wanted.

Clint soon got a good connection. He went to surfer sites and searched for Hilo Hank, who was Henry Francis Goode. He won a minor competition. San Diego. June 12, 2011.

He had the places Tammy had been outside the US from her passport. She had been in France in June and early July, 2011. Unless she knew him from somewhere else he wasn't who they were after.

Sydney Lindsay was Lorraine Lindsay. Sergio would get her passport information – as well as everyone else there.

Eddie Baines was Edward Louis Baines.

He checked on the raffle where Tammy won the vacation. Unless it was just one of those things a local club had, it wasn't registered.

He thought. He checked hospices for AIDS patients in Southern California. There were several. None of them had run a raffle.

This wasn't accomplishing much.

He had another idea. He got the airline ticket numbers from the stubs and unused tickets Tammy had. He went to the police net and asked for full information about the ticket purchases.

They were all bought for cash. Paul Vance made the purchases. They were purchased four days before the supposed raffle win. They were for Tammy Fordham Sheridan – with her passport number for boarding pass issue.

Paul Vance. Thirty four of them. None of whom seemed likely.

She had a draw of a hundred dollars a day. From an ATM card.

He checked the account. Opened by a Peter Vincent.

The killer's initials were P. V.

Was there a ... yes. Eddie had mentioned Phil Vanderhaven, who had set up the raffle and who wanted to marry Tammy. Had he arranged this to ask her to marry him, she laughed in his face or something, he killed her?

Very thin. He wasn't decided if it was her or Sherri he wanted. There could have been others. He would have to do a lot of digging on this one.

Panamá tourists in Bocas del Toro with the initials P. V. He checked immigration. Ponci Vaninni, Italy. Patrick Varness, Ireland. Phryne Velson, Norway.

Vanderhaven was Dutch. Norway wasn't that far. Velson was staying at the Bahia in Bocas Town. Vaninni was at the Sagitario. Varness was with friends in The Bluffs.

Were any of them surfers?

Phryne had brought a board with him.

Clint checked the surfer websites for him. A small line that he was third in a competition in Australia last year. Nothing else.

He called the Bahia. Velson was scheduled to go to Las Tablas. He had taken the early water taxi for Almirante.

He would have time to get to David ... no. Santiago if he took the Panamá City bus. He would go to Las Tablas from Santiago.

Police net: He had taken the bus to Santiago. It had arrived there less than an hour ago. He was on it.

Santiago to Las Tablas ... there would be no checkpoint. He could disappear easily enough. The problem remaining was that he would have to use that passport to get out of the country.

Or to register in a hotel. Clint had an alert for use of the passport.

He might be a lot smarter to go to Las Tablas and disappear from there. It would be a bit too suspicious for him to not get there. Even people with several legal passports had records. If this one wasn't legal, there would be no registration from Norway.

There could be. A trace for a legal alias was in

order.

Clint thought, then called Pedro Placido, the helicopter pilot he used. He said to pick him up in Bocas as soon as possible. Las Tablas.

Clint got off the chopper and said to wait a little while. He may be right back.

Velson was supposed to be at the Big Beach Hotel, just west of Las Tablas. Pedro said he could land on the beach there so they went to land down from the hotel. Clint went inside to meet Velson, who had checked in less than an hour before.

Velson was a dark-haired light complexioned man in his thirties. The passport information came in just before Clint went into the hotel so he already knew Velson wasn't his man. His only passport had been used for France, New Zealand, Thailand and Australia. This was his first trip to this side of the Earth.

Velson was a slender, slightly scruffy man with a Van Dyke beard. He spoke passable English. He had never been to California and didn't want to go there. He might want to go to Hawaii some day. The Heineken beer here was nothing like in Europe.

That was it. Clint headed back for Bocas Town.

Sergio said Ponci Vaninni was Ponci Vaninni. Sherri and Eddie said they saw three people they knew from elsewhere, surfers. Sergio had checked them out and found they weren't any part of anything to do with the murder, though he would keep an eye on one of them. Vincent Porter. There was something a little phony about him.

"He was just a little too stoned," Sherri said. "You could smell the pot in his hair when you got close. Tammy taught me how to do that because it could mean the guy was in some dream world and you couldn't really trust what he said, much of the time."

"Well ... Sherri, do you have a picture of this Phil Vanderhaven?"

"Phil? I think so." She rummaged around in her bag and got a small picture album out. There were twenty or so photos of people, mostly in groups at nightclubs or such. A few were single subjects. Vanderhaven was one.

Phil Vanderhaven was a handsome slender man, about twenty five years old. The picture wasn't very clear, but should be enough.

"Sergio, you can...."

"... see if he's here."

Clint grinned.

"Phil? Why would he...?" Eddie asked.

"Because there was no contest. Tammy was

registered for the flights and at the hotels four days before the supposed drawing for the non-existent raffle.

"I think you'll find he's staying at The Bluffs with some friends, according to the information immigration has."

"Eddie, Sherri? Will you circulate and see if anyone's seen him here? Clint and I will go to The Bluffs to see if maybe he's really got friends there," Sergio suggested. Eddie and Sherri agreed.

Clint and Sergio took the police truck to The Bluffs and went to the house of the supposed friends of Vanderhaven. He was there. He wasn't Vanderhaven. He was a very Irish man with red hair and intense blue eyes and an open friendly personality. He wasn't a surfer type. He was there to write articles for the surfer and tourists magazines. He was more into the backpackers than the surfers.

"Shit! We're back to square zero!" Sergio complained on the way back to Drago. "We can't even get to square one from here!"

"Ain't it the truth! I had it all figured for him. We would have a celebration about how smart and clever I am tonight, then I'd go back to Cusapín and brag about it! As you said, 'Shit!' This gets us less than nowhere."

They parked and went into the restaurant for a

beer. It was just before dusk and they were tired and disappointed.

Eddie came in about fifteen minutes later to announce, "You were right, I think! Phil was here. Some people saw him at the Mondo Taitu last night. In Bocas Town.

"They weren't sure, but the picture looked a lot like him. The picture's two years old, but he looks a lot like that. His hair's not so long now is all.

"We met Irene Fletcher and her latest. We met in Oahu last year. Is it okay for Sherri and me to stay here tonight? We can go back to Bocas in the morning."

"They're the ones who saw Vanderhaven in Bocas Town?" Sergio asked.

"No. That was the German girls, Helen and Gretta. Phil bought them a drink. He dropped a line that he uses, but a lot of surfers use that one. 'Weren't you in Sydney or Hawaii or whatever last June?' kind of thing. They say no, and you say they had to be. There couldn't be two girls that beautiful in only one world. Crap line, you know."

"You can stay. It may be better if he doesn't see you quite yet – if he's still here," Sergio replied. "One victim's one too many!"

Clint and Sergio got into Clint's boat and headed back to Bocas Town. It had been a long day.

"Mondo Taitu?" Sergio asked.

"About nine. Nobody much around before. Maybe Barco later if he's not there. He's probably long gone. I wish Eddie'd gotten the name he's using!"

"Ha! Not the way this one's going. He's got phenomenal luck on his side!"

"Yes. I'll go rest for a couple of hours. Meet at Mondo at nine?"

"Uh-huh."

Clint dropped Sergio at the police dock and went to his place. Judi Lum, his neighbor, was sitting on his deck with Janet and Nick Storie. They caught up on what was going on back in Florida. Nick was now the head of violent crimes in Naples. His son was in Gainesville University, studying computer science. He had already made a couple of inventions and was getting very wealthy. His daughter, Nicole, was studying criminal procedures and forensics sciences.

Clint discussed his case with Nick, who said he was probably right about the killer, but it could be contracted. Surely, Vanderhaven wouldn't be stupid enough to be there in Bocas.

"I have to find motive!" Clint said. "There doesn't seem to be any. Tammy wasn't into blackmail – which there's no evidence of anyhow. He was trying to get either Sherri or Tammy to marry him. He would not ...."

"Hey, stupid!" Judi cried. "Check on his finances! You said that the Sheridan sisters are disgustingly rich! Maybe he's not as rich as he would like everyone to think?"

"But ... why kill her, even if she did turn him down in a nasty way – which wouldn't suit her personality."

"Would the sister marry him?"

"Sherri? She said he's a solid maybe. So did Tammy."

"So Sherri will get all the money, not just half? What do their parents have to say about it?"

"According to my information they're dead. That plane crash out of Lourdes six years ago."

"Get a copy of that will!" Nick demanded. "There may be a lot more to this ... I have a friend who can get that in a flash. You met Pancho. He even came back to stay with you a time or two."

Judi smirked and took out her cell phone. "Manny? Judi.

"Listen. We need to know what the will ... here's Clint."

"Manny? Hi! I just got back from Drago. A girl was murdered there. Tammy Sheridan. Her sister's here. We need to know what the will said that left the girls Midas rich.

"I'll e-mail the info. Five minutes."

He chatted a few minutes, then went to his computer to send Manny Matthews (Actually Marko Bocinni, retired mafia boss from the states) what information Sergio had supplied about the parents. He then spent about half an hour chatting with Judi and the Stories. Ben and Earl, gay neighbor couple, came to fix a quick gourmet meal. Just before Clint headed for the Mondo Taitu and Sergio, Manny sent the information.

Clint read over the sheet and sighed. This was something that gave whoever married Sherri a motive and a half!

"I'll tell you what I think after we find this guy, but it won't be Vanderhaven unless he's a total abject idiot. I have to find a lot about Vanderhaven. I really do!"

"Such as?"

"Such as ... wait until you see what the will said."

"Will? You're back to not making any sense. Tammy left a will?"

"Not that I know of. Her parents did."

They went in. After a few conversations they found several people who saw someone who looked a lot like the picture. He was called Artie. He was from Texas. He was okay if a little crude. Some surfers were, but he seemed more a phony than a real surfer.

Clint asked if he was staying somewhere they knew about. They said the Grand Kahuna, but he was probably already gone. He was in two nights ago. He also went to the Barco Hundido.

They went to the Grand Kahuna. Arthur Finch stayed there two nights and had gone back to Texas yesterday. Yveth, the girl watching the place, said he was a sort of demanding type. He was more like some of the older gringos. He didn't ask for things, he ordered them.

He looked a lot like the picture, but sort of different. The picture looked like a nice enough guy, this one wasn't. This one seemed not to even know his own name. She had called him twice and he hadn't even looked up, then had suddenly said he wasn't listening and what did she want. Once she heard him make a call on his roaming. He was right by the door and didn't know she was inside. He said it was Phil calling.

Clint thought a bit, then said they should go to the station. He wanted to know what kind of information immigration had on Arthur Finch.

"He'll be Vanderhaven?"

"No way! He wants people to think he was. That was a bit too contrived. This whole mess is! Something is off kilter! Badly off kilter!

"I want you to read what the parents' will said. I want to know exactly who Finch is. Everyone says he's a hood type."

Clint called Manny and said he had to know what connections Arthur Finch had to whoever.

"Finch? Arturo Finchesi? I think he had the name changed legally. He wants to get away from Papa's rep. He's another pea. Papa was into some things in Houston, Texas, and was branching out.

We stopped most of it in California, but he's got irons in that fire."

"Hired goon type?"

"Not for money. He's got more than enough. Favors, maybe. Maybe a hit as a lark. He's a killer type like his Pops. Maybe to keep anyone in his new circle from finding out what he really is. He has pretensions."

"So he might be here to kill someone as a favor or because it would stop him from being identified as being what he is?"

There was a pause. "And you wanted a copy of that will. Someone has used or pressured him to kill the girl. The Vanderhaven person."

"I don't think so. I really don't. Someone's trying to make it look like Vanderhaven had it done or did it himself. Question is: Who?"

"Careful, Clint! Could be a double take! Check on exactly where Vanderhaven really is ... I'll do that!"

"This thing was thought out almost all the way. I'm not jumping to anymore conclusions. I think I've been wrong all along. About a lot of things." He and Sergio went to the station where Clint handed Sergio his outline of the will.

Standard opening.

First party: Allen Frederick Sheridan

To my wife, Arlene Fordham Sheridan, all

possessions to be disbursed at her discretion. Should she predecease me, all possessions except exceptions on codicil are to be placed into the charge of my oldest daughter, Tammy Fordham Sheridan for disbursement as she deems fit. Should she predecease me such items are to be tendered to my younger daughter, Sherri Fordham Sheridan.

amend: Two millions of dollars cash are to be first awarded to my younger daughter, Sherri Fordham Sheridan.

Second party: Arlene Fordham Sheridan

Presented as afore stated with the names of Allen Frederick Sheridan and Arlene Fordham Sheridan reversed in position.

"Hmm. So Sherri gets the whole kit and kaboodle now," Sergio commented. "Whoever marries her gets the brass ring."

Clint handed him the list of assets. "It's a platinum ring."

Cash in held accounts: May 1, 2008:
HSBC: $24,894,640.71
1st Federal S&L: $11,673,458.20
Chase: $43,728,977.76

"Eighty million dollars, *in cash*?! Why in unholy Hell would she take a vacation won in a contest?!"

"She was a Valley Girl. It was a smuggin lark, like."

"Sheesh!"

"So. Where is Vanderhaven and who's really behind it?"

"Who's your candidate? This Finch hood?"

"For the actual killing, probably. I want to know who set it up. It could be Vanderhaven, but he's on the back burner for the moment. It could be Baines. He sold the phony ticket. It could be Sherri, but that would seem excessive unless there's something we don't know. It could be from something we don't know diddly about.

"I want to check on a few things. Her lawyer would handle them. Do you have a way to contact her lawyer?"

"It will be on the form. We had to send them a copy of the death certificate."

Clint looked them up. Kline, Donalds, Levin, Murray, Mendez & Associates. There was a phone number. He called.

"I'm with the police in Panamá. A client of your firm, Miss Tammy Fordham Sheridan, was murdered by strangulation here two days ago. I must speak with the person in charge of her account with you. Investigation necessitates further information. You are guaranteed full security of nondisclosure."

"Yes. I heard about that. Tammy was a very nice person. I believe Dan Miller handles the family's legal matters. One moment, please?"

"Dan Miller?"

She laughed. "Yes. There are seven unlisted associates.

"Dan? This is a police officer here in Panamá. About Tammy? Can you spare a few minutes of your valuable time?"

"Thanks, Cindy. I have nothing to do for the next hour or two, but don't tell him that!"

"Oops! He's on the line!"

They both laughed. "I'm Dan. Dan Miller. How can I help you? Tammy was a friend as well as a client. Sort of flaky and sort of fun."

"Clint Faraday. I'm an investigator. This case is weird and complicated. I have to know about anyone who she had any legal dealings with. I have to know if she has a will, particularly one that no one knew about."

"I see. She might still be alive if someone knew about it?"

"It's a distinct possibility. It would be a matter of how it was worded."

"Oh?"

"Was there a clause that would limit what the spouse of the sister could get for a certain time?"

"I see. I think I know where this is going. The parents' will left everything solely in Tammy's charge. Someone wants to get their hands on more than the two million Sherri has, so kills Tammy, then marries Sherri.

"I've checked on the financial situations of several of the people at Tammy's insistence. Might I have checked on the one who killed her?"

"Or hired her murder."

"I see. Finch has a few million, but it is from gangster connections of the father. He isn't the type who has exhibited any desire for more. He is disposed to violence.

"Baines is very comfortable. He seems a real person. It is my understanding he is there with Sherri.

"Leslee – I haven't a clue as to why she had Leslee Annemarie Albins checked – is more than comfortable. She is what we refer to as Valley Girls, but, then, so is Sherri and so was Tammy.

"Phillip Vanderhaven is comfortable, but has some small financial problems. He doesn't seem concerned with money. He has the ability, proven, to get as much money as he wants. He is a very talented sculptor whose art garners as much as half a million a shot – and he's got a short waiting list.

"He's somewhat bisexual. It's not a problem here, though it may seem that it would be to someone not from Southern California. Panamá is not Southern California."

"It's almost part of the culture here. Nobody cares. I doubt Tammy was the type to try to blackmail anyone. My own fourteen year old son tells me about his new experiences, which would *not* happen there. I try not to react like the gringo I was. I act like it's, 'Oh, really? Did you enjoy it?' It's not how I feel I can tell you!"

"If she knew anything about anyone, she would giggle and joke about it with them and would probably tell them something about herself. I feel your son is like that?"

"Yes. He's Indio. They like sex and like to talk and joke about it.

"I guess you can't shorten my suspect list?"

"You asked about a will? I haven't answered specifically?"

"Oh? What?"

"Sherri is going to get the shock of finding she doesn't get anything but the big house here. She already has two million dollars she hasn't spent a nickel of. The house and grounds are on the order of five million more. She'll probably sell that to avoid the taxes. Sherri's would-be will learn that also. Had it been known would Tammy still be alive?"

"Very, very probably. Thanks. Who or what gets the eighty million plus?"

"Six relatives on her mother's side and four on

her father's. They are all ordinary middle class people who deserve it. Tammy was like that. There are several other relatives who don't deserve the time of day and won't be getting it. She always said that a person who didn't try to improve himself and his family wasn't going to be enabled at being a bum! Not by her!"

"I think I would have liked Tammy. I tend to like Sherri and I do like Baines. I do not like Finch, though I've never met him."

"He was here, you know. He left yesterday. We didn't know about him then or he would be sitting in a cell right now."

"He killed her?"

"I'd say so. I want to know who and why."

"Yes. He had no personal motive. I will aid you in any way I can. Feel free to call on me at anytime.

"I really do have a client waiting."

"Thanks again. You've helped a lot in certain areas." He hung up.

"You said a few things?" Sergio asked.

"Sherri doesn't get the millions. A few relatives do. Sherri gets her two million and the house, which is five million more. She won't be able to afford the taxes, so will sell it.

"Finch is the son of a mobster and is a violence freak and a hood, as we suspected.

"Vanderhaven can get half a million for a sculpture. He has a waiting list. He isn't into money. He's – please don't let it bother you – a bit bisexual."

"That's what the bit about Nito was. Who cares?"

"Leslee was checked. He doesn't know why."

"I don't either, not to mention I don't know from nothing who the hell Leslee is."

"I don't either. Tammy must have had a reason to have her checked. They're all a long way from hurting for money or anything else. There has to be something else behind it. Nobody had motive."

"Nobody we know of had motive. Maybe it's someone who doesn't need one. An undetected looney tunes."

"Lord, I hope not! It's what we're left with."

"Sergio, it wasn't some transient thing. If it was, Finch wouldn't be here to kill her. I'm convinced he did.

"What we have to find is what would serve as a reason for him to kill her. It wasn't any thrill killing. Not close to his type! He came here specifically to kill her."

"He came here purposely to kill her and to make it appear as though Vanderhaven had killed her. I've wondered about that. Quite a lot! Why try to implicate Vanderhaven? That's another point that doesn't make any sense!

"Motive is almost always love or money or rage or self-preservation. We don't seem to have any of that here, which leaves a nutcase."

"I can't quite accept that. Nutcases don't go to this degree of planning and setup. They're usually strong reaction killings for some slight or imagined slight that would ... I wonder!"

"I wonder about a lot of things. What?"

"How did Artie Finch get involved with these people in the first place? He doesn't fit, no matter what."

"That was an issue from the start for me. He doesn't fit. How when and why did he become involved?

"I think it's time to talk with Sherri. She might know."

Clint considered. "No. Let me talk with Eddie about this. I don't want to have to tell Sherri that she doesn't get everything yet. If I'm talking with Eddie, that won't come up. If it does, that will tell me something."

Sergio's turn to nod.

"Hi, Eddie! Sherri's not with you?" Clint greeted. He'd waited to approach Eddie until Sherri had gone into the Suites.

"She went to her room. She wants to rest awhile. It's been exhausting, but we had some fun. We didn't learn much of anything except it probably wasn't Vanderhaven the girls saw here in the bar."

"No. It was Artie Finch."

Eddie stared. "Finch? He was here? What does he ... he's not ... Finch?"

"Yes. Finch. He tried to make it look like Vanderhaven was here. We have to know he killed Tammy, but we can't find why.

"What can you tell me about him?"

"But ... Finch? He wasn't part of ... I mean, he was just there a few months ago. He was at ... I think maybe Phil was doing a sculpture of him. We all wondered why. He has the build for it and the looks, but he's crude. He was the type Phil would do before he got to where he had people who contracted for his work. He's the best you ever saw. You think the statue is going to turn around and say hello or something. He gets a lot of money for that.

"Maybe Sherri would know. I think she got drunk or stoned a time or two and ended up in his bed. She's more able to accept those types than most of us. I know Tammy told him she would rather fuck a pig than him.

"Sherri said his father is some kind of mob boss in Texas or something. I think she thought that was exciting."

"Yeah. Some women are attracted to what they consider dangerous types.

"Do you have Vanderhaven's phone number? I'd like to talk with him."

"Yes. I'll write it down for you.

"I suppose Sherri will be relieved in a way. She was saying she was scared shitless that Phil killed Tammy. She was considering marrying him. He might have killed Tammy to get the extra money.

"I told her there was one thing that I knew for certain. It's that Phil couldn't care less about money. He could make an easy five million a year with his sculpture. He did that two years ago!"

They talked a bit more. Clint finally said he had to get to the station and home. He'd talk again later.

Clint called Vanderhaven and told him quite frankly that Finch had killed Tammy and was trying to make it look as if he did it. Where was he the past week?

"The past week? I'm in my studio in Napa doing a figure. A rock idol I won't name yet. She's been with me. It's finished and ready to ship. It's waiting for the truck.

"Where are you? You say Tammy has been murdered? I didn't know anything about it!"

"I'm in Bocas del Toro, Panamá."

"Where Sherri met that Indio she can't stop talking about? She even says she'd pay for a sculpture of him if she thought he'd agree."

"Guillermo? He would be the perfect study! He'd seduce you within five minutes."

"He's gay?"

"Bi. Like almost everyone here. He's with Tammy or whoever wants him. It's how he makes a living."

"Finch tried to make you think that I killed Tammy?"

"He tried to make people think he was you. It was a little overdone. I just wondered why he would try to implicate you, personally."

"I don't have anything to do for a few weeks. I'll come there. I think I want to meet this Guillermo. If he's half of what Sherri and you say he can seduce me. He already has and I'm never met him!

"I'm bi. I make no bones about it. I can come

right away. As soon as I can book a flight.”

“That might be a good idea. I can have you on a flight anytime you’re ready. A friend has a major part of an airline.”

“It’s ... ten fifteen. I can be at the airport by two, packed and ready. Anytime after that.”

“I’ll have Pancho call you and tell you when the next flight leaves. It’ll be to Panamá City. I can have a chopper there to bring you here if it’s not a time when there’s a flight.”

“You have a chopper ready? You must have as much money as our little group!”

“I don’t have much else to spend it on down here.”

Clint soon called Pancho DeGulio. Pancho had recently visited him on the comarca. He said he’d have the regular two ten flight held if Phil couldn’t get there in time. He would call Phil and make the arrangements.

It was just five in Bocas. Vanderhaven could come on the morning flight from Panamá City.

Some people were due for quite the surprise!

He called Manny and asked some questions. He got the answers he expected.

Tomorrow he might get the final answers. His serious suspects were now down to just three. Reactions would show whether or not the one he was sure was behind it really was.

He went to his house and took Nick and Janet to dinner at Refugios. They had a fun night. They went back and to bed about midnight.

"He does look like the picture," Sergio noted. "He's a very handsome sort. You say he's bi, so Guillermo will like him if his personality is as you say.

"I don't know why you wanted him here or why it matters if he is bi."

"I think I know what's behind this. It's not money from the killer's perspective, but is from the perspective of the one who made the plan. It's shock time for a couple of people!"

They went to Vanderhaven as he came inside to introduce themselves. They had him booked at the Bahia.

They went out to the police truck they would use as a taxi. Guillermo was standing there talking with a pretty gringa who was there to catch her flight out. She looked tired and very satisfied. Clint grinned and asked if her stay in Bocas had been pleasant. She said she never knew it was possible for anything to be as pleasant as this one had been.

Sergio introduced Guillermo to Vanderhaven, who was obviously taken with him. Clint winked at Phil and said, "Guillermo, would you be willing to pose for a sculpture, nude?"

"Okay. Will it take long? I have to make a living, same as anyone else "

"I'll pay for your time. Will a million dollars cover it?" Phil said, getting into the spirit of things.

"Twenty five dollars per day and we sleep together. It's my regular rate."

"Ah, yes. You are a whore, according to Sherri."

"The twenty five, yes. The sleeping because I think you'll be plenty fun. I've had nothing but women for two weeks and can use the change."

They got in the back of the truck to head for the Bahia Hotel. They joked all the way. When Guillermo had Phil settled in his room they came back downstairs to head for Chitres for a delicious typical lunch.

While Guillermo and Phil were still upstairs Sergio asked what the hell this was about. Clint said it was to set a mood.

"A mood about sex? I don't get it!"

"I want the bisexual bit to be totally expected and natural. I need to know the reaction of one person."

"Baines? Sherri?"

"Not really. Finch."

"Finch?"

"Finch. Manny arranged for him to come back

like it or not. I think he'll tell us what I almost know as fact."

"Who hired him?"

"He wasn't actually hired. He was tricked. It will make him go ballistic when he sees that."

"And he'll give us the one behind the whole sick scheme. We can hope."

"Sick is a good description, I'd say."

Guillermo and Phil came back down. They had their lunch, then Guillermo said he and Phil would go to some places Guillermo knew about.

Clint had talked with Guillermo and told him to try to see that Sherri and Baines didn't know Phil was there. It was to be a surprise when they got together tonight at seven thirty. They would all meet at Ben and Earl's for a gourmet dinner. Phil and one other person were the big surprise. Guillermo asked if he was to not sleep with Phil. Clint said that was up to them. Phil was no part of the real problem. Just be totally as natural as he always was. If something happened with Phil, that was fine. If it didn't, it didn't.

Clint and Sergio went to the airport to meet Finch two hours later. He was surly and just short of threatening. He claimed he was as much as kidnaped and forced to come here.

"You were here a couple of days ago to kill Miss Sheridan," Sergio countered. "This is your chance to get some understanding of what was done to you and by whom. You will answer to justice for that, but there is no reason to make things any worse than they are.

"We can let you stay in the Sagitario at our expense or can hold you in a cell. Whichever, it is your choice. You'll find we're a lot more civilized than the bunch you were raised around.

"As stated, you were used and manipulated. I would tend to think you'd be most interested in knowing who did it and how it was done.

"Understand one other thing. You will get a sentence of perhaps six years here that will begin immediately or you can be sent back to the United States with all evidence. There you will face two or three years of courts and pleas, meanwhile being held in a cell. You will then face a sentence of twenty years. You will have been out and free for the last fifteen of those years should you prove to have the intelligence to see it.

"You will believe that your father can arrange something in the United States. Bear in mind that he couldn't even keep you there right now. Wonder who and what we have that nullifies what he has. Act accordingly."

Finch stared at Sergio a moment, then looked at Clint. "Is he for real? I can stay at a hotel when I have a murder, er, manslaughter charge against me if I promise not to cause trouble or run or whatever?"

"Yup! As real as they come!" Clint answered. "There's no lesser plea here. Manslaughter is murder. This wasn't particularly heinous so you're already facing a minimum charge. If you argue, it gets worse. This is an island. There's nowhere to run.

"I think you'll give us what we need. I doubt you appreciate being put into a situation where only you could lose.

"I'll ask only one other thing. You don't go anywhere you might be seen by anyone who's connected with your little California clique."

"Gonna spring them on me to see who pisses in her pants?"

"Something like that. Do you like paella?"

"If it's made right!"

"By a master chef. Be ready to go to dinner tonight at about seven thirty."

"Cool."

"Nobody says that anymore."

"I do."

Sergio took him to book into the Sagitario. Clint went home to get things ready. Earl would make what was probably the best paella any of them (except Judi, Sergio, Guillermo and Clint) had ever tasted. They knew and were friends with Earl and Ben. They and hundreds of others had already pronounced it the best.

Clint found Sherri and Eddie and said they had a big surprise dinner tonight. Be ready at seven!

They said they'd be there! They had never enjoyed a vacation as much as this.

"That's a terrible thing to say with my sister dead, but it's true. She would have wanted us to enjoy this place."

"A murder seems so ... out of place here," Eddie said. "I feel guilty for having fun."

"Well, we'll clear that up as fast as we reasonably can. We know who killed her. It's a matter of filling in a few details," Clint said.

"Vanderhaven, wasn't it?" Sherri asked.

"No. His alibi is as solid as a granite tombstone. He couldn't have possibly done it."

"He could have hired it, I suppose?"

"Anybody could arrange it to where they would seem safe.

"See you at seven! You know where Ben and Earl live?"

He told them how to get there and went to his house to get things ready.

Ben and Earl had a big table that seated twelve. Earl was a master chef by occupation. Ben also was a damned good cook.

Nick and Janet were seated on one side with Guillermo and Phil next to them. Finch and Earl were on the other side opposite Nick and Janet. Clint was at the foot of the table, Ben at the head. Eddie and Sherri would be seated in the center of that side. Sergio was on Clint's end.

Everyone was seated except Earl and Ben. Sherri and Eddie would be there in minutes. Ben poured some special wine and was about to give a welcoming speech when Sherri and Eddie came in.

Sherri let a small yelp escape when she saw the people seated at the table. Eddie looked very puzzled. He raised an eyebrow at Clint.

Ben poured them wine and went back for the welcoming speech.

"Welcome all! I'm Ben. I've been introduced to all of you except Miss Sheridan and Mr. Baines. Clint arranged this dinner party so he could do a Nero Wolfe or something as silly. We all know who killed Tammy." He nodded at Finch, who looked confused and a little nervous.

"Anyhow, it's a chance to show off for Earl and me.

"Oh! Sherri and Eddie, Earl is my lover. He's a master chef. You're going to eat the best paella any of you ever tasted tonight! He's even outdone himself!

"So! Dinner is served! Bon appetite!"

Earl rolled in an enormous tray with a huge platter of paella and plates. If it tasted a third as good as it smelled it was exceptional.

It was. Clint had to agree Earl had outdone himself.

When they had finished the dinner Clint stood and said dessert would be served shortly.

"I would like to ask a few questions if I might.

"For instance, how did Artie get introduced to your group?"

"His father wanted a sculpture of him. He said Artie was the only really handsome man in the family for years," Phil answered. "Seeing his body was like looking into a mirror, I had to agree.

"Excuse me if I'm vain. An artist has a right to be!"

He leaned against Guillermo, who laughed and hugged him.

"We're both shot right out of the saddle by Guillermo," he said.

"My god! Get a room!" Sherri snapped.

"We did. Where do you think we were all afternoon?" Guillermo fired back.

"How can you be ... I mean, you don't care if everyone knows?" Finch asked.

"Nobody cares, except they're all jealous of me for being the one with Guillermo," Phil replied.

"This isn't the states. If you've got an itch, what difference does it make which hand you scratch with?" Judi said.

"Is that what's behind you doing it?" Sergio asked. "You were pressured into it because you had slept with ... Phil?"

"And Tammy had said she would rather fuck a pig?" Clint added.

He didn't say anything for a few seconds, then said, "Because my father would have me hit if he knew. That's how he is. I would be an abomination against god and would disgrace the entire family."

"She blackmailed you into it? Why not just get rid of her?"

"She has pictures. Pops would get them."

"Er, Tammy had pictures of you? You killed her anyway!" Sherri cried.

"No. You had the pictures," Sergio said. "You

didn't know about the will she had made.

"Clint? Read her the important parts?"

Clint picked up the sheets by his plate.

"Due to some things I've learned, I am making this last will and testament before my lawyer, Mr. Miller.

"Should something happen to me, all assets of the estate I'm charged with administering will be divided as follows in this text.

"There's a list of ten people who receive everything except the estate house. You already have two million, noted here."

"Will you verify that you were pressured and coerced into this by Miss Sherri Fordham Sheridan, Mr. Finch?"

"Oh, yeah!"

"Will you tell us about it?"

"Sherri and I had a little fling awhile back. A couple months or so. I was there because Phil was making a statue of me. He's damned good! I look like I'll smile and ask if you want a quickie any minute!

"Anyhow, Phil and I were together and I was naked and he made it plain he was interested in ... some things.

"I had never done anything like that, but he's handsome as hell and is a really good guy and it might be fun.

"I can tell you it was!

"There were a lot of pictures of me. Some of them had him in them. They were mostly for the statue and some for memory, you know? We were both naked and he was kissing me in one. One was really sort of, you know, a little too close.

"Sherri saw a couple like that on a table when she was there and stole them.

"See, I had tried to get Tammy into bed. She was kind of nasty about it and said I was a pig or something. She made me feel like a clod of shit! All I wanted was a little recreation for fun! I never said I loved her or any of that shit!

"Anyhow, Sherri said her sister had all the money and wouldn't even give her a little to buy a car she wanted, but she could get it all, and, after all, Tammy had cut me down to a stub that everybody knew about and made me a big joke to all her friends.

"I noticed that all her friends would stay away from me. It was pretty plain that she was mouthing off against me.

"Sherri made up some kind of plan about a contest that Tammy would win. She would get a free vacation. I said that was stupid. She could make her whole life a big vacation with what she had.

"Sherri said it would be a lark. It was the kind of

thing her sister couldn't turn down. She'd been to all those places and knew Tammy would go ape-shit in Bocas, what with people like Guillermo.

"I can see why Phil likes him. I think I could even maybe ....

"Anyhow. She said I looked just like Phil from a distance. Nobody here would know either of us. Tammy had refused to marry Phil so people would think he was pissed and had killed her.

"She wasn't the first I killed. Only the first woman.

"I thought it would be a way to get even for her making a joke out of me. I agreed. I did it. Here I am."

"So. It boils down to your father being a sadistic monster who would kill his own son for something as silly as having a romp with another man. Tammy rejected you. Her sister wanted her dead. You had killed before. You did it," Sergio said.

"Yeah. that's about it."

"I must now charge you with causing an unwarranted death. You will serve three years if you do not contest the charge."

"That would be stupid, seeing I admitted everything right here in front of a dozen people!"

"Okay. I'll arrange for your incarceration, Monday, so you have four days to prepare yourself. I'll not hold you if you'll remain here and cause no further problems."

"Thanks. I wish people in the states were half as human as you!"

"Miss Sheridan, I hereby charge you with premeditated murder. You will serve eight years should you not contest the charge."

"Are you out of your mind?! *I* didn't kill her! *He* did!"

"Under your plan and pressure, thus you are guilty of causing your sister's death through premeditation."

"I damned well will contest it! You can't prove anything!"

"We don't have to prove it. You have to disprove it. I do not see any possibility of that here.

"Mr. Finch will not run nor try to avoid his sentence, thus I will allow him his freedom until time to begin sentence. You are not of the same disposition and have stated clearly that you will contest the charges, thus you will be incarcerated until a hearing where the judge may suggest bail or incarceration.

"That can wait until after dessert! I saw Ben's famous cold key lime/pineapple pie. I would not miss a chance at a small sample of that!"

They chatted, all except Sherri, who sat in a corner and refused to speak with anybody until she talked with her lawyer.

Sergio told her she could spend this one night at her hotel, but she would have to be jailed the next day. She left.

"She'll pay someone to get her out of Panamá before morning," Phil warned.

"Yes. I know."

"I don't get it! You can't let her get away with this!"

"She won't," Judi said. "Clint arranges these things so Panamá doesn't have to feed and house those type for years. She'll head for Costa Rica. Sergio will send all the testimony to California. It will show she as much as admitted it. She had solid witnesses against her who showed she planned and caused the death of her sister. She was in California at the time of the planning and the execution of the plan, ergo, she's now their headache. She doesn't have eighty million to spend on lawyers. She'll be convicted."

"She'll stay away from California is all."

"But she has no money unless she goes there to claim it."

"So. She has the option of facing it here, running to California where she'll be charged, or not being in either place. She'll end up a street person somewhere. She has no skills. Maybe a prostitute," Finch said. "Maybe she can go to Pops, who will have her hit because of what she claims about me. He wouldn't blink."

"I suppose they'll want your testimony in California. I'll allow you to go," Sergio said.

"No way! I'm convicted here and will have to stay! I can do three years standing on my head.

"Will they let me stay here after?"

"If you have been rehabilitated sufficiently and not declared undesirable."

"Well, I suppose I am, but so long as it's not declared as such...?"

"Clint can arrange it."

"Well, I have a sculpture to begin. I'll need to study the subject very carefully before I can do it justice. I think I'll have to begin the research immediately!" Phil announced.

"Oh, bullshit! You already did some careful studies. You said so. This afternoon!" Judi pointed out.

"That was preliminary. I'll have to get into a much more intense mode for what will be the crowning achievement of my life and career!"

"Well, the crowning achievement of the year maybe. Let's go. I need some rest," Guillermo said.

"Ha! You're not going to get much," Sergio warned.

They went out, laughing and joking.

Nick and Janet said they'd heard Clint was like

that, but Sergio had learned the lesson very well indeed!

Clint said he just wanted to get back to his wife and family. He had to get some rice and flour for her mother first.

Clint and Tyna got out of his boat at his deck. Judi saw them and waved from her own deck. She called that she'd be right over.

Clint and Tyna would stay three or four days, then go to their mountain place near Quebrada Tula for the next several months.

Judi came in and said it was good to see them. She and Tyna would fix a gallon of the fine coffee from a friend in the mountains. Coffee that good wasn't available anywhere. Chico grew and ground it himself. It was from a few plants by his cabin. He grew the commercial stuff, but this was a special plot of special coffee he shared with his closest friends.

Clint would go into Bocas Town to talk with people he knew. He would visit Sergio and Ben and Earl.

He went by the Golden Grill. In the past he would have stopped to chat with the regulars, but two had died and he didn't know the newer ones. He waved at the three he knew and went to the station.

Sergio was transferred to the main offices in

Panamá City. He was head of education in police procedures, violent crimes. He was rated the top officer in the country in cases solved.

He hadn't wanted the job. He wanted to stay in Bocas, but he was the best. They needed him.

He claimed Clinton Faraday had taught him most of what he knew, that it was Clint who solved many of his cases.

Clint wasn't an officer. He was a special aide. He couldn't be conscripted into a teaching job.

Sergio had been in the position only a week when a case came up that had the entire force stumped. He had done computer research that limited the suspects to six people. Solid alibis reduced that to four. Non-suspect witnesses eliminated two more.

He had two. He remembered when Clint had found a receipt in a bag in a garbage can, so went to evidence and through what they had.

Nothing – but there was a toothpick on a platter that had served sausages and olives.

DNA test time! DNA from either suspect would show they had been in a place they couldn't hope to explain.

Sergio personally arrested "Cuestick Carlos" for the murder. Carlos had been paid by the husband to kill the wife, who had a business and bank account in her name. He wanted to marry a woman he was having a long-term affair with.

"Clint Faraday taught me that the simple fact an object is too small for prints doesn't mean it holds no evidence. A DNA chain is one hell of a lot smaller than a toothpick or fingerprint!"

Naldo Vicente, the new head of violent crimes, grinned as Clint handed him back the report. "I was here for two months. Sergio taught me more in that time than I had learned in two years of university."

"Sergio is one hell of a good officer. Panamá needs more like him.

"I lost track of the last case here. I was going to follow it on the computer, but it slipped by."

"Oh, yes. Vanderhaven has moved here permanently. He made a pinkish marble statue of Guillermo that looks more alive than you could believe."

"Guillermo? He's still with Guillermo? That's hard to believe!"

"Oh, no. He's now living with Osiria, that beautiful Indigeno woman. Your wife's cousin, I believe. He and Guillermo are very close friends. I think Guillermo is the only man he's been that close to.

"The Sheridan woman managed to get ten percent of what cash she had in the bank in California by bribing a banker here – or in

Ecuador. She's there now. They gave her amnesty when she bought a place. She can leave the hundred fifty thousand she has in the bank as a CD and live on the interest there if she's careful.

"Finch worked some odd deal where he's a personal attendant to a woman who owns some big almacen in Panamá City. He drives her around and sleeps with her. He gets to stay out of jail in house arrest. It helps that her brother is a bigshot politician! You know how that one works here.

"Did you know Manny's son is graduating from Panamá University next year with top honors? He's studied medicine and is going to be in charge of all those hospitals and clinics you, Manny and Judi built.

"Sergio told me Manny was a crime lord in the states under a different name. I'm never to mention that to anyone but you and Judi and that strange Dave character.

"Dave was here last week. He's very spry for an eighty year old man. He's going to some place in the middle of the comarca in The Darien or somewhere. I'm thirty three and wouldn't do that!"

"It's what he does. We Indios take care of him even if he doesn't need it."

"He is popular with them. Every kid in the area calls him Abuelo Dave."

They chatted awhile, then Clint went back to his place. Judi was telling Tyna about the statue of Guillermo. There was a woman Clint didn't know sitting with them.

"... by the name of Rodgers said he's pay a million dollars for it, but Phil said it wasn't for sale. Some major arts magazine had a writer here to do an interview. She said she was in love with Guillermo from just looking at that sculpture. It was really fun when Guillermo walked in in person.

"You know Guillermo! He stripped and let her take pictures of him standing beside the statue. She took about fifty more than she could possibly need.

"Hi, Clint! I'm telling Tyna about Phil's statue of Guillermo. It's about the only thing anyone's talked about since he unveiled it last week.

"This is Leslee Albins. She was a friend of Phil and Eddie and the rest. She had to come here because of what she'd read about the sculpture. She likes the place, but more in the mountains. She's going to buy a vacation house above Volcan."

"It's beautiful there. It's quiet and cool. Judi was showing me the orchids around this place when I got here. My place has a lot of them. Dave, a friend of yours – oh, yes. He brought all these orchids – found one he said is very rare. It's beautiful! It's an Odontoglossum that he said is only found in Northern Peru. He found two others near my place last year. He said a lot of things that aren't found here are.

"It took a minute for that one to register.

"Cymbidiums should go riot there! I have a collection I can bring to plant. They do well in Northern California, but not too well in the southern end. They need cool nights the year-around.

"I'm excited. I never knew anything about Panamá other than the canal. It's heaven! The people are so nice, and they aren't impressed by Miss Rich Bitch Hoity-toit! I'm just another woman who might be a friend.

"I read about you back home. You're a very famous person in some circles. You're just 'My friend, Clint' here! I love it!

"Now that I'm running down, what are my chances with Guillermo? I have to meet him! Judi says she'll introduce us."

"If you've got the money, he's got the time," Clint replied. "He makes no bones about him being a gigolo."

"I saw that boy that he's supposed to be his father. He's only seven years old and is going to be a hunk! He'll be a gigolo by the time he's sixteen, I'll bet. I'll bet Guillermo was!"

"Try twelve or thirteen," Judi said. "He's honest about it."

"Yes. That's charming in its own way. I met that Sanders woman. She's a prostitute, but I'll bet he's like her. She says she's a nympho. Not many people can make the thing they like best their living!"

"There's no question of what Guillermo likes best," Tyna said with a laugh. "He's a sex addict in heaven!"

They talked and joked for a long time, then Judi took Leslee to meet Guillermo.

Clint sighed. He was as lucky as Guillermo. He had made what he liked best in life, the thing that would always have his interest, his main occupation.

It wasn't about money. Not that kind of thing. It was what he was born to do. He had more money than he knew what to do with. He still worked his ass off like any other Indio on the comarca. He was content. He had a place.

None of those people from the states had a place. They spent their lives trying to find one.

He'd found it after fifty years of searching!

He held Tyna close and brushed her hair with his lips. Twenty two years and he loved her more than ever.

He had it all! Eat your heart out!

C. D. Moulton's works are available on most major outlets as printed or e-books. CD writes the CD Grimes, PI, mysteries, the Det. Lt. Nick Storie mysteries, the Clint Faraday mysteries, the Flight of the Maita science fiction series, books on orchid culture and many others of many types. Mystery, adventure, intrigue, science fiction, humor, fantasy, paranormal, mild erotica, and factual.